The Hunt for
Anakin Skywalker

GAME BOOK

**The galaxy is yours.
Be a part of**

STAR WARS®

EPISODE I

ADVENTURES

. . . and more to come!

STAR WARS®

EPISODE I

ADVENTURES

GAME BOOK

The Hunt for
Anakin Skywalker

Dave Wolverton

SCHOLASTIC INC.

New York Toronto London Auckland Sydney
Mexico City New Delhi Hong Kong

ISBN 0-439-12989-3

12 11 10 9 8 7 6 5 4 3 2 1   0 1 2 3 4 5 6/0

Printed in the U.S.A.
First Scholastic printing, February 2000

YOUR ADVENTURE BEGINS

For the full story behind your adventure, read up to page 36 in your Star Wars Adventures novel, *The Hunt for Anakin Skywalker.* Or begin here.

You are Sebulba, Gondry, Khiss, or Djas Puhr. The *Adventure Guide* contains the rules of Star Wars Adventures. You must follow these rules at all times.

Recently on the planet Datar you captured several Ghostling children to sell as slaves. However, once you got them to Gardulla the Hutt's fortress on Tatooine, someone freed them. You suspect that it was four slave children disguised as Jawas. Your seeker droid has caught the scent of one of those children, and now you plan to catch the boy.

Your plan is simple: follow the boy and catch him.

Choose your character. Every character has unique talents that are listed on each character card. You can use Power three times on this adventure.

You start this adventure with your Adventure Point (AP) total from your previous adventure, or 1000 AP if this is your first adventure.

Be careful. If you mess this up, every crime lord in the galaxy will ridicule you!

YOUR ADVENTURE:

THE HUNT FOR ANAKIN SKYWALKER

"Do you see him?" the seeker droid asks in its monotone. Its black casing is sleek and stealthful.

You are running through the market at the Mos Espa Spaceport, in the rush of the afternoon crowd. The twin suns of Tatooine are blinding. Sweat trickles down your face and back.

A hundred meters ahead of you, a blond boy is ambling along. Suddenly the boy stops, as if alerted to your presence. He starts to turn.

The seeker droid drops to the ground, taking cover.

You must avoid detection, with or without Power.

To avoid detection (without Power): Roll the 20-dice to leap for cover behind a dewback. Your roll# + your stealth# + your skill# is your adventure#.

If your adventure# is equal to or more than 13, add the difference + 10 to your AP total. A giant dewback glances at you, but he's the only one who sees you. You may proceed.

If your adventure# is less than 13, subtract the difference from your AP total. The boy spots you and bolts for the nearest building!

To avoid detection (with Power)*: Choose your Hide Power. Roll the 20-dice to hide behind a dewback. Your roll# + your Power# + your Power's high-resist# + your stealth# is your adventure#.

If your adventure# is equal to or more than 13, add the difference + 6 to your AP total. You're as hard to spot as a gravel-maggot hiding under a Hutt. You may proceed.

If your adventure# is less than 13, subtract the difference from your AP total. Anakin rushes for the nearest building.

*NOTE: This counts as one of three Power uses you are allowed on this adventure.

The boy runs into a cantina. You recognize the spot instantly. It's called the Racer's Edge. Lots of racers hang out there, but not you. No one you know would be caught dead in there.

Well, you think, *if I am caught in there, I'll be dead soon enough.*

You hesitate for a second, hoping that the boy will run back out. He doesn't. You consider calling your friends to back you up before going in, but you don't want people to think that you're a coward.

You rush inside, taking your chances.

The cantina is cool. Plants growing from pots along the ceiling keep it moist. The evening band won't show up for hours. Creatures from fifty worlds are here — Podracers and their managers and pit crews, moisture farmers, and criminals.

You scan the room, looking for the boy. But he's nowhere to be seen.

The bartender glances up at you and your droid. "Hey," he growls. "No droids."

He points at the seeker droid.

You toss him a coin. "Just passing through," you say. "We're looking for someone."

An old enemy glances up at you — Skarrish Kor. He has yellow skin and pointed ears. The right side of his face is nearly covered by a black metal mask that contains a glowing red mechanical eye.

Two of his pit crew are with him — both

of them Devaronians, with hairless heads and protruding horns.

"Hey," Skarrish Kor calls, "looks like you found someone — or maybe *we* found *you*!"

One of his Devaronian sidekicks reaches down warily, unhooking the strap to his blaster. The other puts his leg out into the aisle, to make sure you don't run past.

You can try to talk your way past these goons with or without Power, fight your way past without weapons, or fight your way past with weapons.

To talk your way past Skarrish Kor (without Power): Roll the 20-dice to convince him that you are in a dangerously bad mood. If charm is one of your talents, your roll# + your charm# + 3 is your adventure#. If charm is not one of your talents, your roll# + your charm# + your stealth# is your adventure#.

If your adventure# is equal to or more than 14, add the difference + 15 to your AP total. You snarl at Skarrish Kor and say, "Buy me a drink, Skarrish, and I might let you live." Skarrish, impressed by your courage, nods at the bartender, who offers you a drink. You grab it and continue searching the cantina.

If your adventure# is less than 14, subtract the difference from your AP total. You snarl at Skarrish Kor and say, "Buy me a drink, Skarrish, and I might let you live." Skarrish snarls back, "Dead men don't drink." You must try to fight your way past with a weapon, or without a weapon (page 13).

To talk your way past Skarrish Kor (with Power)*: Choose your Persuasion Power. Roll the 20-dice to convince him that you're not his enemy. Your roll# + your charm# + your Power# + your Power's high-resist# is your adventure#.

If your adventure# is equal to or more than 13, add the difference + 15 to your AP total. You say, "Skarrish Kor — just the man I've been looking for. Let me buy you and your boys a drink. I've got a business proposition for you." Skarrish Kor is so surprised that he lets the bartender set up the drinks. As he does, you excuse yourself, and go look for the boy.

If your adventure# is less than 13, subtract the difference from your AP total. You offer to buy Skarrish a drink and talk business, but he merely growls, "The only business we need to handle is best done with blasters." You must fight him with or without a weapon (next page).

*NOTE: This counts as one of three Power uses you are allowed on this adventure.

To fight Skarrish and his men with a weapon: Choose your weapon. Roll the 10-dice. Your roll# + your weapon's short-range# + your weaponry# is your adventure#.

If your adventure# is equal to or more than 9, add the difference + 10 to your AP total. You draw your weapon and fire. Skarrish Kor frantically ducks, scared out of his wits. His henchmen raise their hands and back off. You proceed to hunt for the boy.

If your adventure# is less than 9, subtract the difference from your AP total. You miss Skarrish Kor. The blaster bolt hits the table, blowing up his drink. He sputters in surprise. You may fire at him again. Roll the 10-dice again. Your new roll# + your weapon's short-range# + your weaponry# + 1 is your new adventure#.

If your new adventure# is equal to or more than 9, add the difference + 5 to your AP total. Skarrish Kor frantically ducks, scared out of his wits. His henchmen raise their hands and back off. You proceed to hunt for the boy.

If your new adventure# is less than 9, Skarrish Kor returns fire. Roll the 10-dice.

If the roll is equal to or more than 6, he misses. Go back to "Roll the 10-dice again" and repeat.

If the roll is less than 6, he hits you! Fortunately, his gun is set on stun, and you will wake up in a few minutes. Subtract 1 from your strength# for the rest of the adventure. Then you exit the cantina. Go to the sentence that starts, "The seeker droid whisks down the road" (page 14).

To fight Skarrish and his men without a weapon: Roll the 10-dice. Your roll# + your strength# + your stealth# is your adventure#.

If your adventure# is equal to or more than 7, add the difference + 12 to your AP total. You kick the table that Skarrish Kor and his men are sitting at. The table flies up and knocks them all over. As they're trying to pick themselves off the floor, you proceed to hunt for the boy.

If your adventure# is less than 7, subtract the difference from your AP total. You kick at Skarrish Kor's table and manage to knock over one of the Devaronians. Now the rest of the gang is on you. You must fight them one at a time. You must knock out all three opponents before you can proceed. Roll the 10-dice again. Your new roll# + your strength# + your stealth# is your new adventure#.

If your new adventure# is equal to or more than 7, add the difference to your AP total. You knock one of the three attackers over. Go back to "Roll the 10-dice again" and repeat until you have defeated all three attackers.

If your new adventure# is less than 7, subtract the difference from your AP total. Go back to "Roll the 10-dice again" and repeat until you have defeated all three attackers.

The seeker droid flies to the back of the cantina. "Our quarry has gone through this door." You open the door, race out the back of the cantina, and find yourself on the next block.

Give yourself 50 AP points for making it through the cantina.

The seeker droid whisks down the road and drops to a culvert. It's too small for either the droid or you to crawl through. You realize that the boy has gone underground, but that the culvert has to come out somewhere.

Across the street is a dome-shaped building with a transmission tower atop it. From up there, you should be able to see half of the city.

You charge across the street and try to climb the dome.

To climb the dome: Roll the 20-dice. Your roll# + your stealth# + your strength# is your adventure#.

If your adventure# is equal to or more than 12, add the difference + 6 to your AP total. You climb up the dome quickly and quietly.

If your adventure# is less than 12, subtract 5 AP from your AP total. You slide down the dome like a rock in an avalanche and must try again. Go back to "Roll the 20-dice" and repeat until you reach the tower.

You reach the top of the dome and easily climb the transmission tower. From there, you can see over the buildings and across the street.

You look for the blond boy. You may track him without Power or with Power.

To find the boy (without Power): Roll the 10-dice. If tracking is one of your talents, your roll# + your skill# + 2 is your adventure#. If tracking is not one of your talents, your roll# + your skill# is your adventure#.

If your adventure# is equal to or more than 6, add the difference + 5 to your AP total. You spot the boy's blond head bobbing between some dewbacks as he makes his way up the busy street. You may proceed.

If your adventure# is less than 6, subtract the difference from your AP total. Go back to "Roll the 10-dice" and repeat until you've found the boy.

To find the boy (using Power)*: Choose your Find Power. Roll the 10-dice. If tracking is one of your talents, your roll# + your skill# + your Power# + your Power's low-resist# + 1 is your adventure#. If tracking is not one of your talents, your roll# + your skill# + your Power# + your Power's low-resist# is your adventure#.

If your adventure# is equal to or more than 7, add the difference + 5 to your AP total. You spot the boy's blond head bobbing between some dewbacks as he makes his way up the busy street. You may proceed.

If your adventure# is less than 7, subtract the difference from your AP total. Go back to

"Roll the 10-dice" and repeat until you've found the boy.

*NOTE: This counts as one of three Power uses you are allowed on this adventure.

Once you spot the lad, you realize that the fastest way to reach him is to leap across the rooftops. But you have to do it without him seeing you! You may try it without Power or with Power.

To leap across the roofs (without Power): Roll the 10-dice to make your leap. If jumping is one of your talents, your roll# + your strength# + 3 is your adventure#. If jumping is not one of your talents, your roll# + your strength# + 1 is your adventure#.

If your adventure# is equal to or more than 7, add the difference + 5 to your AP total. You leap to the next roof, and then climb down the gentle slope of a dome to get to the ground. You may proceed.

If your adventure# is less than 7, subtract the difference from your AP total. You leap for the roof, but miss. In the resulting fall you sprain your steering arm. Subtract 1 from your navigation# for the duration of this adventure. Now roll the 10-dice again to leap to the next roof. Your new roll# + your strength# + 3 is your new adventure#.

If your new adventure# is equal to or more than 7, add the difference to your AP total. You make it to the next roof, and may proceed.

If your new adventure# is less than 7, subtract the difference from your AP total. Go back to "Now roll the 10-dice again" and repeat until you make the leap.

To leap across the roofs (using Power)*: Choose your Jump Power or your Reflex Power. Roll the 10-dice to leap over the roof. Your roll# + your strength# + your Power# + your Power's mid-resist# is your adventure#.

If your adventure# is equal to or more than 8, add the difference + 5 to your AP total. You bounce from rooftop to rooftop like a ball. You may proceed.

If your adventure# is less than 8, subtract the difference from your AP total. You hit the edge of the opposite roof — and then stumble. You fall off the edge and grab the ledge just in time to save yourself. Now you must pull yourself back up. Roll the 20-dice. Your new roll#

+ your strength# + your stealth# is your new adventure#.

If your new adventure# is equal to or more than 13, add the difference to your AP total. You pull yourself up onto the roof. You may proceed.

If your new adventure# is less than 7, subtract the difference from your AP total. You're still hanging there. Go back to "Roll the 20-dice" and repeat until you're on the roof.

*NOTE: This counts as one of three Power uses you are allowed on this adventure.

You carefully make your way down to the crowd and begin closing the distance between you and the boy. You imagine how good it will feel to finally catch him. Gardulla will reward you handsomely, and once the boy is questioned, he will lead you to his accomplices.

The crowd here is thick. A bunch of Gamorreans is wandering in front of you, looking at a merchant's batch of oversized swords. Jawas are under your feet. Eopies plod through the crowd looking for any scraps of food that people might drop.

You are nearly upon the boy when a Jawa bumps into him. Suddenly the boy ducks into the crowd.

You leap up, but can't see him. The seeker droid whips through the air, and you run to catch up. The seeker veers behind a stall where a vendor sells power generators for vaporators.

You round the corner and see a Jawa racing from the seeker. The Jawa is wearing a simple brown robe, like any other Jawa, but it doesn't walk like a Jawa.

You race around a corner after him, and suddenly find yourself in the scrap market, where hundreds of Jawas are milling in the streets. There are droids and people all around, and huge displays of junk thrown out on tarps on the ground. You see a tangle of landspeeders and eopies.

But in that sea of Jawas, where has the boy gone?

You quickly spot a Jawa running for his life in a very non-Jawa way. You shout over your comlink to warn your accomplices: "The boy is running for the Podracer hangar. He'll be hiding in there."

The seeker thrums in the air through streets made narrow by the influx of tourists. To your right, crates have been stacked to form a drink stand, where dozens of thirsty Jawas climb up to get mugs filled with a dark brew. To your left, a Jawa merchant has stacked old generators forming a huge wall.

Suddenly, from the high counter off to the right, a Jawa throws a bucket of dark fluid over its shoulder.

The syrupy stuff hits the seeker droid full on, smearing all over it.

An accident! you think.

Black juice drips from the droid. You recognize the bitter scent of ganno. The stuff makes your sinuses burn as if you were breathing acid.

Oh no! you think. *It will ruin the seeker!*

The seeker buzzes to a halt.

You shout to the seeker droid, "Are you all right?"

"There's ganno juice on my olfactory sensors. I can't smell a thing!" the droid says.

You rush to save the droid.

*　*　*

To rescue the droid, you must wipe the ganno juice off before it drips into its housing and short circuits the electronics.

To rescue the droid: Roll the 10-dice. If repair is one of your talents, your roll# + your skill# + 2 is your adventure#. If repair is not one of your talents, your roll# + your skill# is your adventure#.

If your adventure# is equal to or more than 7, add the difference + 15 to your AP total. You quickly wipe the ganno juice off with your sleeve. The droid looks safe for the moment. You may proceed.

If your adventure# is less than 7, subtract 40 AP from your AP total. Ganno is dripping like syrup all over the circuits. By the time you get it all off, some damage has been done. You'll have to pay to get the seeker fully repaired — when you have time.

You are busy cleaning the droid when you hear a cry of outrage from the Jawas at the drink stand. For half a second, you had imagined that the Jawa was simply tossing away some bad juice.

But now you realize that the Jawa had

hurled a whole bucket on purpose. It wasn't an accident. It was an attack!

One of the children did this!

You whirl and draw your blaster, glancing up at the stand. But there have to be thirty Jawas there, and they all look alike to you.

You study them feverishly.

"Who threw that?" you demand, hoping that the Jawas will point out the culprit.

One of the Jawas spins.

"Want seconds?" a girl shouts. A second bucket of ganno juice hurtles through the air.

You can choose to evade the ganno juice without Power or evade it with Power.

To evade the ganno juice (without Power): Roll the 20-dice to leap from the path of the bucket. The number you roll is your roll#. If jumping is one of your talents, your roll# + your strength# + your stealth# + 1 is your adventure#. If jumping is not one of your talents, your roll# + your stealth# + 1 is your adventure#.

If your adventure# is equal to or more than 14, add the difference + 9 to your AP total. You duck from the attack so quickly, one would think you were dodging bullets. You may proceed.

If your adventure# is less than 14, subtract the difference from your AP total. Blech! The ganno juice hits you in the face, temporarily blinding you and making your sinuses swell shut. If tracking is one of your talents, it will no longer be one of your talents for the rest of this adventure.

To evade the ganno juice attack (with Power)*: Choose your Reflex Power. Roll the 20-dice to dodge from the path of the liquid. Your roll# + your stealth# + your Power# + your Power's low-resist# is your adventure#.

If your adventure# is equal to or more than 13, add the difference + 7 to your AP total. You dodge the flying liquid with the grace of a Jedi Master. You may proceed.

If your adventure# is less than 13, subtract the difference from your AP total. Ganno juice hits you in the face, temporarily blinding you and making you feel like you're having the worst allergy attack in the galaxy. If tracking is one of your talents, it will no longer be one of your talents for the rest of this adventure.

*NOTE: This counts as one of three Power uses you are allowed on this adventure.

Before you can use your blaster, your attacker jumps down from the boxes, leaping behind the booth. You think about going after her, and run behind the booth.

Dozens of Jawas are there, but you don't see the girl among them. You know she has to be hiding somewhere!

"Master," the seeker droid calls. "Look over there!"

You glance across the scrap market to see a lone Jawa running toward the hangar. Negotiating through the crowd will take time. You have a better idea.

You see a nearby landspeeder. You think you might get by faster if you went around on the side street. Next to the speeder is an orange creature that looks like a three-eyed octopus. It is bartering with a Jawa for spare parts. The orange alien seems desperate for money, but is also intensely occupied.

You may try to steal the landspeeder from the alien (with or without Power), or you may try to take it through deception (with or without Power).

To steal the landspeeder (without Power): Roll the 10-dice to climb into the landspeeder without being seen. Your roll# + your stealth# is your adventure#.

If your adventure# is equal to or more than 6, add the difference + 6 to your AP total. This alien may have three eyes, but they're all looking off in other directions! You may proceed.

If your adventure# is less than 6, subtract 5 AP from your AP total. One of the alien's eyes pops out on an eyestalk and stares right at you! "Excuse me, creature," the alien says, "what are you doing with my landspeeder?" You will have to attempt to deceive the alien (next page).

To steal the landspeeder (with Power): Choose your Infiltration Power. Roll the 20-dice to sneak into the speeder. Your roll# + your Power# + your Power's mid-resist# + your stealth# is your adventure#.

If your adventure# is equal to or more than 13, add the difference + 6 to your AP total. This alien may have three eyes, but he must have blinked them all at just the right moment! You may proceed.

If your adventure# is less than 13, subtract the difference from your AP total. The alien says,

"Excuse me, fellow citizen of the galaxy, but you seem to have wandered into my landspeeder!" You will have to use deception to get this alien's landspeeder (below).

*NOTE: This counts as one of three Power uses you are allowed on this adventure.

To deceive the alien (without Power): Roll the 20-dice to convince the alien that you are interested in buying the landspeeder, and want to take it for a test drive. If charm is one of your talents, your roll# + your charm# + 2 is your adventure#. If charm is not one of your talents, your roll# + your charm# is your adventure#.

If your adventure# is equal to or more than 13, add the difference + 10 to your AP total. The remarkably honest orange alien says, "I would sell it to you, but I must warn you that it is not very reliable. Please, take it for a test drive first." You may speed away!

If your adventure# is less than 13, subtract the difference from your AP total. The alien is suspicious. "Why would anyone want to buy this piece of junk?" the alien asks. "Are you insane?" You must talk harder to convince the alien that you want the speeder. Go back to "Roll the 20-dice to convince the alien" and repeat until you've gotten the landspeeder.

To deceive the alien (with Power)*:
Choose your Persuasion Power. Roll the 20-dice to convince the alien that you wish to take the vehicle for a test drive. Your roll# + your charm# + your Power# + your Power's low-resist# is your adventure#.

If your adventure# is equal to or more than 13, add the difference + 15 to your AP total. "Please," the alien says, "take my landspeeder for a test drive — though I fear it will not be good enough for you!" You may proceed.

If your adventure# is less than 13, subtract the difference from your AP total. "This being must be mad to want my lowly landspeeder!" the alien cries. You must talk harder to convince the alien that his landspeeder is good enough to be worth some money. Go back to "Roll the 20-dice to convince the alien" and repeat until you've gotten the landspeeder.

*NOTE: This counts as one of three Power uses you are allowed on this adventure.

You pilot your newly acquired landspeeder through the crowded streets of Mos Espa. *What a piece of junk,* you keep telling yourself. *I hope no one sees me in it!*

You whip around the side streets until you near the far side of the Jawa scrap market. The streets are very crowded. Jawas are setting up stalls everywhere.

Eopies mill through the crowd. Battered droids amble about, displaying themselves for any who bother to look.

Normally, this street is pretty clear. But occasionally the Jawas come in large numbers.

You reach an intersection. A dewback ridden by Jawas is crossing the road in front of you. You have to stop for the giant reptile. This could take a while. The Jawas on it are dragging a sled through town, loaded with an old rocket engine.

The seeker droid shouts at you, "I'll follow the boy. You catch up!"

You nod. The droid blurs off through the intersection.

You shout at the Jawas, "Hurry up!"

You quickly check the setting on your blaster, and move it to *stun*. When you catch the boy, you don't want to kill him. Gardulla will want to spend a few days torturing him first. You set the blaster in the seat beside you, where you can grab it quickly.

The dewback stops ahead of you. Four Weequays on rontos are coming from the opposite direction. They clog the intersection. The Weequays shout at the Jawas to move their dewback. The Jawas shout in return.

One of the Weequays raises an old blaster rifle and shakes it over his head, threatening. The Jawas on the dewback draw their own weapons.

"Get out of my way!" you scream at the whole lot of them. You wonder if it would be faster to back up and try to swing around the block.

Suddenly there is a movement to your right. A Jawa rushes from the crowd beside you, reaches into the landspeeder, and grabs your blaster.

"Hey, nice blaster! Can I borrow it?" the Jawa asks. Only the voice isn't a Jawa's — it's a boy's!

The boy grabs the blaster and fires into the front Weequays' ronto.

"Hey, lucky shot!" the kid says. He tosses the blaster back to you, then rolls underneath the landspeeder.

The ronto isn't wounded. A blaster set on stun won't hurt it. But it *will* make it furious. It trumpets in rage, swinging its great head. It knocks over a fruit stand. The Weequays on its back begin to shout. They cling to the rampaging monster for dear life.

The street fills with screams of terror. The Jawas begin firing their ion blasters into the air, trying to drive the ronto off.

"What?" you ask. It all happened so fast!

You grab your blaster by the barrel. It's still hot, and sears your fingers. You flip it in the air and take it by the handle.

You try to look under the landspeeder, to see where the pesky kid is hiding.

A bolt tears through the seat next to you. The Weequays are shooting at you! They think that *you* shot their ronto.

You look up to assess the danger. The ronto swings its mighty head, slams into the dewback, and turns its angry eyes on your landspeeder. It charges! The Weequays on its back take aim at you.

You have to get out of here quickly!

To evade the charging ronto (without Power): Roll the 20-dice to drive quickly. The number you roll is your roll#. If navigation is one of your talents, your roll# + your navigation# + your vehicle's speed# + 1 is your adventure#. If navigation is not one of your talents, your roll# + your navigation# + your vehicle's speed# is your adventure#. (Note: If you sprained your arm earlier, remember to subtract 1 from your navigation#!)

If your adventure# is equal to or more than 13, add the difference + 10 to your AP total. You drive better in reverse than you do going forward! You may proceed.

If your adventure# is less than 13, subtract the difference from your AP total. There's a Wookiee in your way. Looks like you'll have to drive that ronto away (below).

To evade the charging ronto (with Power)': Choose your Reflex Power or your Evasion Power. Roll the 20-dice to veer from the path of the monster. Your roll# + your vehicle's speed# + your Power# + your Power's mid-resist# is your adventure#.

If your adventure# is equal to or more than 13, add the difference + 7 to your AP total. You shoot out of the crowd like a ship into hyperspace.

If your adventure# is less than 13, subtract the difference from your AP total. You crash into a pesky protocol droid. Looks like you'll have to drive the ronto away (below).

*NOTE: This counts as one of three Power uses you are allowed on this adventure.

To drive the ronto away: Choose your weapon. Roll the 10-dice to stun the ronto. Your roll# + your weapon's short-range# + your weaponry# is your adventure#.

If your adventure# is equal to or more than 9, add the difference + 12 to your AP total. The blaster hits the huge ronto right between the eyes — you think. The ronto turns around, bellows in fury, and decides to go take his wrath out on a helpless droid. It's now out of your way, and you may proceed.

If your adventure# is less than 9, subtract the difference from your AP total. You accidentally knock a Weequay off the top of the ronto! Go back to "Roll the 10-dice" and repeat until you get that ronto.

Your landspeeder stirs up a cloud of sand and dust as it whips back through the narrow streets, faster than any ronto could run. You grip your blaster.

"Oh, I can't wait to get my hands on those kids!" you mutter.

As you back up, you watch the street.

You hope to see the boy who blasted the ronto in the first place. He should be huddled in the dirt road beneath your landspeeder. But as you back up, you don't see him.

Did the kid run off through the crowd while I was distracted? you wonder.

You look around wildly for any sign of the fleeing child, but don't see him.

The ronto is still rampaging. Now the dewback roars in anger and begins to drag the huge engine off in a rush. The intersection is in chaos.

You back around a corner, chuckling with delight. You can't help but admire any kid who can cause so much trouble.

Your seeker droid comes whizzing back through the crowd. It confirms, "The boy is heading for the Podracer hangar. He'll be hiding in there."

You grin wickedly at this good news. The hangar is a familiar place. No doubt the silly child will try to hide in the cockpit of one of the Podracers. "Perfect! Let's go!"

The seeker screams through the air as it races after the boy. You see flames sputter in it, and something ignites. Oily gray smoke is coming out of your seeker droid.

Oh no, you realize. *Some of that ganno juice is dripping into the droid's circuits. Ah well, the droid has almost served its purpose!*

Blue sparks erupt from the droid.

You watch it in rising concern as it veers through the streets, until it reaches the Podracer hangar. As you reverse thrusters and bring your landspeeder to a stop, you hear the whine of engines from inside the hangar. Perhaps one of your racing foes is checking his engines.

The seeker droid hovers by the door for a moment, smoke billowing from it.

"Master," the droid shouts. "In here!"

The droid whips into the shadows of the hangar, calling, "Halt! Halt!" The suns of Tatooine are so bright that you can't see inside.

You stop the landspeeder, leap to the ground, and firmly grip your blaster. You rush to the door just as you hear the whirring engines of a Podracer. Inside the enclosed room, the noise is like the sound of a thousand storms all at once.

You run to the door and look in. There is a brilliant explosion not far ahead.

You see a pinkish beam of light, the energy binders on a Podracer, rushing toward you at incredible speed!

The Podracer screams toward the hangar door, but the door isn't open wide enough. The engines on the racer are enormous, and only a pair of sturdy control cables attaches them to the pod. The Podracer will never fit through that door!

It's coming right at you. Instinctively you throw yourself to the ground.

There's a tremendous *boom!* as the engines slam into the pour-stone walls of the hangar, then burst *through* to the other side!

You're not quite sure how it happened. Most Podracer engines would have never made it through. The housing on those engines was long ago reinforced. They were *designed* to ram into other Podracers. Those huge engines are weapons.

You manage to avoid getting caught in the beam of the energy binders — a fate that would have left you numb for hours. And you also manage to keep from getting pulverized by the cockpit. But that's where your luck stops.

One of the Split-X stabilizing vanes, a small wing really, catches you at the waist.

Suddenly you find yourself hurtling down the roads of Mos Espa, clinging to the engine of the Podracer. You are feeling *very* dizzy and bruised . . . but you have to hang on!

To cling to the Podracer: Roll the 10-dice. Your roll# + your strength# + your skill# is your adventure#.

If your adventure# is equal to or more than 8, add the difference + 10 to your AP total. With muscles strengthened by sheer terror, you cling to the Podracer.

If your adventure# is less than 8, subtract 15 AP from your AP total. You fall off the massive engine and go bouncing through Mos Espa. Go to the line, "You fall from the Podracer engine" (page 40).

The Podracer hurtles down the bright streets of Tatooine, racing through the

Jawas' scrap market. The buildings of Mos Espa rear up on both sides of the road. People scream and duck, and eopies flee in terror.

The driver reverses thrusters, trying to slow down. You shout some curses at him. You pull yourself laboriously up the vane, then crawl from the vane to the top of the engine housing.

"I'll kill you kids!" you scream. You see the Steelton cable that connects the engine to the cockpit. *If I can just pull myself along that cable back to the cockpit,* you think, *I'll be able to stop them!*

But hanging on to this engine is job enough for the moment!

The driver swerves to miss an eopie that wanders in front of him. He veers left around a ronto and goes screaming toward a landspeeder. The passengers all duck just as the driver revs the engines of the repulsorlifts, so that the Podracer gains altitude. He manages to fly over the landspeeder without knocking anyone's head off. He hits his thruster and veers right around a corner. The whole Podracer tilts at a sixty-degree angle. The right engines almost scrape the ground, and for a moment your feet actually kick up some dust.

There is a boy clinging to the outside of the Podracer. Wind whips his Jawa robe, so that you can see his face. You wish that you could get a good look at the driver, too. "Get him off of there!" the dark-haired boy screams.

"I'm trying!" the driver shouts.

He reverses thrusters, effectively slamming on the brakes. You're thrown forward, but you expected the maneuver and easily adjust.

You grab the control arm that attaches the cables to the engine. You snarl in rage and begin to laboriously climb onto the Steelton cables!

The boy speeds right around another corner, then flies back over the Jawa market. With his altitude adjustment so high, he clears the Jawas' heads nicely.

The fellow shakes his cane at the driver and shouts, "Hah! Missed me!"

You're not deterred by any maneuver that the driver tries. You crawl closer.

The driver reaches a large empty square back at the hangar. He slows the thrusters, and banks hard to the right. The Pod-racer's engines spin a tight circle, and the right engine dips so low that it almost skims the ground. You're nearly thrown on your back.

The force on the Podracer is tremen-dous. Dust and sand rise all around in a flume that reaches into the sky. It is like being at the center of a blinding sand-storm. Grit gets into your teeth and nose and eyes.

Blindly, you cling to the cable arm for your life.

Suddenly you feel something hit your feet. The boy is opening the vents on the Podracer! Fire rushes out, burning you! You let go.

You fall from the Podracer engine and go flying over the ground, and land in a pile of fresh dewback fodder.

It smells terrible, but quickly puts the fire out.

You raise your head, and shake your muck-covered fist in rage. You glare at the retreating Podracer.

"Aaaagh!" you shout. A mere *human* is driving that Podracer. A child is driving that

Podracer! The kid has already blown through the wall of one building, and now is racing it through the streets of Mos Espa.

Only one human in the galaxy has ever successfully piloted a Podracer, and even that boy has never won a race. Human reflexes aren't quick enough.

For half a second, you wonder if it could be Anakin Skywalker piloting the vehicle.

But it couldn't be. Anakin Skywalker isn't stupid enough to drive a Podracer through a wall. Nor would he be so reckless as to try to fly the thing through Mos Espa.

No, it has to be some crazy, desperate kid who knows that if you catch him, he'll be in BIG trouble.

You imagine the precious Podracer slamming into a wall at 800 kilometers per hour.

Part of you wishes it would happen. At least you'd be rid of that pesky kid.

You run back into the Podracer hangar and leap into the most likely machine: a sleek Podracer owned by a racer named Brant Rumble.

You climb into the cockpit and flip the

controls. The telemetry and control console light up. The Tradium power fluid levels are full; coolant levels look to be within safety range. Stabilizers and altitude adjusters seem functional.

You flip the power to the repulsors. The repulsorlift motors began to hum. The cockpit and engines shudder, then lift into the air.

You rev the engines. You know that if you give them too much fuel, they will flame out. But you want to catch those boys now!

To start the vehicle: Roll the 20-dice. If navigation is one of your talents, your roll# + your navigation# + your vehicle's speed# + 2 is your adventure#. If navigation is not one of your talents, your roll# + your navigation# + your vehicle's speed# is your adventure#. (Note: If you injured yourself earlier, remember to subtract 1 from your navigation#.)

If your adventure# is equal to or more than 13, add the difference + 9 to your AP total. You burst out of the Podracer hangar so fast, it feels as if you've left your stomach behind.

If your adventure# is less than 13, subtract the difference from your AP total. Flames shoot from the back of the engine and then the engine makes a clunking noise. You must wait for a second while the excess fuel clears from your fuel lines, then try again, more slowly. Go back to "Roll the 20-dice" and repeat until you've got the vehicle started.

You rev the engines, hurtle into the streets, and race through the Jawa market. Tailing the thieves is easy.

The other Podracer has knocked over market stalls, banged into walls, smashed vehicles, and otherwise created havoc. It leaves a cloud of yellow dust thick in the air, as if a desert sandstorm was blowing into town.

You reach a Y intersection where the streets are swept clean of dirt. All of a sudden, you lose the trail.

You raise your head over the duraplex windscreen of Brant Rumble's Podracer, trying to smell spent fuel. That would tell you which branch to take.

To find the path of the Podracer: Roll the 10-dice. If tracking is one of your talents, your roll# + your skill# + 2 is your adventure#. If tracking is not one of your talents, your roll# + your skill# is your adventure#. (Note: Remem-

ber to subtract 1 from your skill# if you had
ganno juice thrown on you earlier.)

If your adventure# is equal to or more than 7,
add the difference + 10 to your AP total. The
odor of spent fuel in the air is as foul as a
Gamorrean's breath. You veer to the left and
proceed.

If your adventure# is less than 7, subtract the
difference from your AP total. You career in
the wrong direction, but soon recognize your
mistake. You turn left and connect back to the
proper road.

The road ahead soon shows its typical
signs of wear and tear. The boys on the
stolen Podracer have crashed into buildings, slammed into droids, and destroyed a
couple of landspeeders.

You whip past Gardulla the Hutt and
her Gamorrean guards, staring at the re-
mains of a wrecked landspeeder. The wreckage is really cool! There are pieces of
metal everywhere, and the whole landspeeder is crunched together and folded
up like a sandwich. Gardulla has been
badly scorched, and you see some market
stalls on fire.

The boys must have vented the flames from the engine again. You sort of wish that you could stop and look at it all. But there's no time.

Since the boys have cleared a path for you, you hit your throttle and whip down the street.

A vendor in a market, a big Trandoshan, sees you coming. He's mad, and he decides to take his wrath out on you.

He raises a huge blaster rifle and snaps a quick shot!

You can choose to evade the shot without Power or evade it with Power.

To evade the Trandoshan sniper (without Power): Roll the 20-dice to veer from his path. If navigation is one of your talents, your roll# + your navigation# + your vehicle's stealth# + 2 is your adventure#. If navigation is not one of your talents, your roll# + your navigation# + your vehicle's stealth# is your adventure#. (Remember, if you were injured earlier, subtract 1 from your navigation#.)

If your adventure# is equal to or more than 13, add the difference + 15 to your AP total. You blur past the Trandoshan sniper so fast, he sprains his neck trying to look at you!

If your adventure# is less than 13, subtract the difference from your AP total. The Trandoshan shouts, "Blow this out your exhaust assembly!" and blasts a hole through your power steering servo assembly. Steering this Podracer will be extra hard for the rest of the adventure. Subtract 1 from the vehicle's speed# and stealth# until this adventure is over.

To evade the Trandoshan sniper (with Power)': Choose your Reflex Power. Roll the 20-dice to veer from the path of the blaster fire. Your roll# + your vehicle's stealth# + your Power# + your Power's low-resist# is your adventure#.

If your adventure# is equal to or more than 12, add the difference + 15 to your AP total. You go screaming past the Trandoshan shouting, "You couldn't hit a womp rat if it was sitting on your nose!" The Trandoshan jumps up and down in rage, throws his weapon on the ground, and stomps on it.

If your adventure# is less than 12, subtract the difference from your AP total. The Trandoshan shouts, "Take that!" and blows a hole through your power steering servo assembly. Steering this Podracer will be extra hard for the rest of the adventure. Subtract 1 from the vehicle's speed# and stealth# until this adventure is over.

*NOTE: This counts as one of three Power uses you are allowed on this adventure.

The buildings towering on each side of the narrow street and the walking pedestrians make the course as dangerous as any that has ever been raced. This road is at least as challenging as Arch Canyon.

You round a corner. Through a sandy haze, you see the fiery engines of a Podracer down the street, crawling at a Hutt's pace.

Stupid kids. They're puttering along. One boy still dangles from the outside of the racer.

People and animals lunge for safety out of their path. The boys have to go slow. But the streets are clear behind them.

To catch up to the Podracer: Roll the 20-dice to speed up. If navigation is one of your talents, your roll# + your navigation# + your vehicle's speed# + 1 is your adventure#. If navigation is not one of your talents, your roll# + your navigation# + your vehicle's speed# is your adventure#. (Remember, if you were injured earlier, subtract 1 from your navigation#, and subtract 1 from your vehicle's speed# if it's been damaged.)

If your adventure# is equal to or more than 13, add the difference + 10 to your AP total. You've fulfilled the need for speed.

If your adventure# is less than 13, subtract the difference from your AP total. You're still a little far behind. Go back to "Roll the 20-dice to speed up" and repeat until you've caught up.

You whip toward your quarry and rush up on the Podracer from behind. The kids in Jawa robes glance back in terror.

The driver veers far to the left, to let you pass. A plan suddenly comes to mind.

You veer right toward a building and bank hard into the turn, so that for a moment the Podracer rises up at a seventy-degree angle, hurtling just over the surface of the dome. You fight the controls in this deadly maneuver.

To bank the Podracer (without Power):
Roll the 20-dice. If navigation is one of your talents, your roll# + your navigation# + your vehi-

cle's speed# + your strength# + 2 is your adventure#. If navigation is not one of your talents, your roll# + your navigation# + your vehicle's speed# + your strength# is your adventure#. (Remember, if you were injured earlier, subtract 1 from your navigation# and/or strength#, and subtract 1 from your vehicle's speed# if it's been damaged.)

If your adventure# is equal to or more than 15, add the difference + 10 to your AP total. You bank the corner so beautifully that you just wish Jabba the Hutt were here to see it!

If your adventure# is less than 15, subtract 30 AP from your AP total. Your right engine slams into the building, breaking through the pour-stone. You've broken a fuel line, and fuel is venting from the engine. You must try to repair the damage! Roll the 20-dice. If repair is one of your talents, your new roll# + your skill# + 2 is your new adventure#. If repair is not one of your talents, your new roll# + your skill# is your new adventure#.

If your new adventure# is equal to or more than 12, add the difference + 10 to your AP total. You manage to shut down the ruptured fuel line and route some fuel from the reserve tank.

If your adventure# is less than 12, subtract the difference from your AP total. Go back to "Roll the 20-dice" and repeat until you fix that engine.

You blur past the boys. You shoot out of town, over the desert. The land opens up, becomes a desert flat with sandstone monoliths rising here and there from the desert floor, like giant guardians turned to stone.

You spin in a wide circle. You've raised an enormous dust cloud behind you. Through the drifting yellow cloud you see the boys still driving out of town toward you.

You grin cruelly. You know how to play upon the darkest fears of your foes.

This boy thinks he's running away from death, you realize. *What will he do if he sees it racing toward him?*

The buildings of Mos Espa form canyon walls to the boys' right and left, walls so narrow that they can't turn the big engines around. There's no escape for them! The Podracer slows, and one of the kids jumps off.

The driver has seen the danger, you think. *He's hoping to let his little friend escape. How noble of him. But it won't do any good.*

You open up your throttle and aim Brant Rumble's Podracer straight at the slowed vehicle. The driver sees your maneuver and suddenly speeds up, as if hoping to reach the edge of town before he's caught.

But he's too late. You sweep forward.

Your engines roar. The sound echoes from the city walls. Wind blasts your face.

To aim for the other Podracer: Roll the 20-dice to get in position. If navigation is one of your talents, your roll# + your navigation# + your vehicle's stealth# + 1 is your adventure#. If navigation is not one of your talents, your roll# + your navigation# + your vehicle's stealth# is your adventure#. (Remember, if you were injured earlier, subtract 1 from your navigation#, and subtract 1 from your vehicle's stealth# if it's been damaged.)

If your adventure# is equal to or more than 12, add the difference + 11 to your AP total. There's no escape for him now. You may proceed.

If your adventure# is less than 12, subtract the difference from your AP total. You're still a little off. Go back to "Roll the 20-dice" and repeat until you're headed straight for him.

You're closing on him fast, a red gleaming beast surging through clouds of drifting sand. The boy veers right, and keeps his Podracer hugging the side of the street. You swerve to meet him.

The boy clutches the control handles, unsure what to do. He's afraid that you'll crash into him, that both vehicles will explode. You want him to be terrified. If he dares to stop, you'll be able to leap out and catch him. If he tries to veer off too fast, he'll crash.

Either way, you'll get what you want.

Fear is your best weapon. You slow your Podracer slightly, raise a blaster, and aim over the boy's head.

To fire: Choose your weapon. Roll the 20-dice to fire. If targeting is one of your talents, your roll# + your weaponry# + your weapon's far-range# + 1 is your adventure#. If targeting is not one of your talents, your roll# + your weaponry# + your weapon's far-range# is your adventure#.

If your adventure# is equal to or more than 13, add the difference + 5 to your AP total. The blast just misses the other Podracer — you've had the desired effect. You may proceed.

If your adventure# is less than 13, subtract the difference from your AP total. Your shot misses, and the force of the recoil causes you to veer slightly off direction. You must right your course. Roll the 20-dice. If navigation is one of your talents, your new roll# + your navigation# + your vehicle's stealth# + 1 is your new adventure#. If navigation is not one of your talents, your new roll# + your navigation# + your vehicle's stealth# is your new adventure#. (Remember, if you were injured earlier, subtract 1 from your navigation#, and subtract 1 from your vehicle's stealth# if it's been damaged.)

If your new adventure# is equal to or more than 13, add the difference to your AP total. You are back on track. You may proceed.

If your new adventure# is less than 13, subtract the difference from your AP total. You're still a little off. Go back to "Roll the 20-dice" and repeat until you're back on track.

The boy swerves to his left, into the middle of the street. He hits the thrusters, and bends down.

Suddenly, your jaw drops open in terror. You had only meant to scare the kid. But the boy is going to kill you both!

He's ducked his head. Perhaps he expects to die, and doesn't want to see the moment coming. Or maybe he's afraid he'll get shot if he pokes his head above the dashboard.

"Aaaagh!" you shout.

You aim the blaster over the duraplex windscreen of Brant Rumble's Podracer and blast the ground in front of the boy.

You throw down your weapon and swerve to your far left. The engines twist on their energy binders as you bank against the side of a dome.

The two Podracers hurtle toward one another, engines screaming.

There's not enough room to pass! you realize.

Suddenly, the boy pops his head back up, hurls something, and banks to his left.

The Podracers have just enough room to clear one another on the right.

But something is falling through the air!

You recognize goggles and metal spanners — just as the jet engines on Brant Rumble's Podracer suck them all in.

The right engine grinds to a halt and takes a nosedive into the hardpan of Mos Espa. Dirt and soil spray high into the air and the whole city shudders with the sound of the exploding engine.

The Steelton control cable snaps off at the engine arm. The remaining engine hurtles on, dragging the cockpit behind it at hundreds of kilometers per hour.

You fight the controls. Without two engines to keep the cockpit stable, yours swings on its lone cable like a pendulum. The Pod grazes a peddler's stand to the left, slams wide over to the right, smashes into a big cleaning droid, and veers back left.

You've got to stop this vehicle!

To keep from crashing (without Power):
Roll the 20-dice. Your roll# + your navigation# + your vehicle's speed# + your strength# is your adventure#.

If your adventure# is equal to or more than 14, add the difference + 30 to your AP total. You manage to shut off the repulsorlifts so that the Podracer drops to the ground like an anchor, while you turn off the engines. You escape without serious injuries.

If your adventure# is less than 14, you manage to turn off the repulsorlift on the cockpit, so that it drags behind the lone engine like an anchor. However, you don't slow the engine in time, so the cockpit drags too much. The Steelton control cable snaps, and the cockpit goes rolling end over end. You're going to get hurt! Proceed to the section that starts, "If you have crashed" (next page).

To keep from crashing (with Power)': Choose your Reflex Power. Roll the 20-dice. Your roll# + your vehicle's speed# + your Power# + your Power's high-resist# + your navigation# is your adventure#.

If your adventure# is equal to or more than 14, add the difference + 30 to your AP total. You effortlessly wrestle with the control — turning off the power to the repulsorlifts on the Podracer, steering perfectly, and downing the thrusters on the engine so that you don't crash.

If your adventure# is less than 14, your control cable snaps and the cockpit goes hurtling through the streets — crashing into buildings, smashing innocent droids, and scattering junk and debris over the road for two kilometers. Proceed to the section that starts, "If you have crashed" (below).

*NOTE: This counts as one of three Power uses you are allowed on this adventure.

If you have crashed, roll the 10-dice.

If you roll 1: You've sprained an appendage and won't be able to scratch where it itches for a week. Subtract 20 AP from your AP total.

If you roll 2: You've twisted your leg and have to crawl away from the wreckage. Subtract 30 AP from your AP total.

If you roll 3: You'll never be able to drive on Tatooine again! Subtract 40 AP from your AP total.

If you roll 4: You've broken your nose, and can't kiss anyone for a month! Subtract 40 AP from your AP total.

If you roll 5: All of the twisting and turning as the Podracer flips end over end makes you throw up. Your friends will be reminding you of this for years to come. Subtract 35 AP from your AP total.

If you roll 6: You get knocked unconscious and wake up so swollen you look like you're Gardulla the Hutt. Subtract 40 AP from your AP total.

If you roll 7: The medic droids rush to your aid. They throw you in a bacta tank for a couple of hours. It will take you years to pay off the medical bill. Subtract 30 AP from your AP total.

If you roll 8: The medic droids rush to your aid. They throw you in a bacta tank for a couple of hours. It will take you years to pay off the medical bill. Plus, the money you were carrying fell out of your pocket — so now you're broke! Subtract 40 AP from your AP total.

If you roll 9: The Podracer crashes into Watto's junkyard. He steals the most expensive parts, then claims that Jawas did it. Subtract 30 AP from your AP total.

If you roll a 10: You've sprained an appendage and won't be able to scratch where it itches for a week. You've twisted your leg and have to crawl away from the wreckage. You'll never be able to drive on Tatooine again! You've broken your nose, and can't kiss anyone for a month! All of the twisting and turning as the Podracer flips end over end makes you throw up. The medic droids rush to your aid and throw you in a bacta tank for a couple of hours. It will take you years to pay the bill. Plus, the money you were carrying fell out of your wallet! Then your mother learns about it from the HoloNets, and calls you up. She cries and tells you that you're an embarrassment to your species! But she promises to do her best to keep loving you anyway, and she enrolls you in a driver's safety class. Subtract 100 AP from your AP total.

When the Podracer finally stopped, a cloud of dust rose in the street so thick that it looked as if a storm had blown in off the desert.

The boys you've been chasing are long gone. But you're not done with them yet. Already, a scheme is forming in your mind — one that will give you your vengeance.

You have failed to capture the pesky little thieves, but at least you're alive.

You can try again tomorrow. Add 300 AP to your AP total.

To read the end of this adventure, please turn to page 83 of your Star Wars Adventures novel *The Hunt for Anakin Skywalker.*